# the Big Bag

Vivian French

Illustrated by Chris Fisher

16902

Published by the

Penguin Books Ltd, 27 Wrights Lane, London W8 5TZ, England
Penguin Books USA Inc., 375 Hudson Street, New York, New York 10014, USA
Penguin Books Australia Ltd, Ringwood, Victoria, Australia
Penguin Books Canada Ltd, 10 Alcorn Avenue, Toronto, Ontario, Canada M4V 3B2
Penguin Books (NZ) Ltd, 182–190 Wairau Road, Auckland 10, New Zealand

Penguin Books Ltd, Registered Offices: Harmondsworth, Middlesex, England

Published in Puffin Books 1994
10 9 8 7 6

Filmset in Bembo Schoolbook Monotype

Printed in England by Clays Ltd, St Ives plc

Hector was getting ready to go out.

"Where are you going?" asked his dad.

"I'm going to go to the very middle of the woods," said Hector. "I'm going to catch my dinner."

"Well," said his dad, "be careful."

Hector went round to see Hattie.

"I'm going to go to the very
middle of the woods," he said.
"I'm going to catch my dinner.
Will you come too?"

"All right," said Hattie. "Let's
catch some grasshoppers."

Hector and Hattie went to see
Harry.

"We're going to go to the very
middle of the woods," said Hector.
"We're going to catch our dinner.
Will you come too?"

"All right," said Harry. "Let's
catch some snails."

Hector and Hattie and Harry
went to see Hester.

"We're going to go to the very
middle of the woods," said Hector.
"We're going to catch our dinner.
Will you come too?"

"All right," said Hester. "Let's
catch some wriggly worms."

Hector, Hattie, Harry and Hester
ran through the long grass.

"Are we nearly there?" asked
Hattie. "I'm getting hungry."

"It's not far now," said Hector.

"Good," said Hattie.

Hector, Hattie, Harry and Hester walked underneath the bracken.

"Are we nearly there? asked Harry. "I'm getting hungry."

"It's not far now," said Hector.

"Good," said Harry.

Hector, Hattie, Harry and Hester crept under the brambles.

"I'm getting VERY hungry," said Hester. "Are we nearly there?"

"It's not far now," said Hector.

"Good," said Hester.

Hector, Hattie, Harry and Hester reached the very middle of the woods.

"Oh!" said Hector.

"Where are the grasshoppers?"
asked Hattie.

"Where are the snails?" asked
Harry.

"Where are the wriggly worms?"
asked Hester. "I'm VERY hungry."

Hector scratched his nose. "Perhaps we should go home again," he said.

"NO!" said Hattie and Harry and Hester. "We want to have a rest!"

"All right," said Hector, and they all sat down.

Hector and Hattie and Harry and
Hester closed their eyes.

Hector and Hattie and Harry and
Hester went to sleep.

At the other end of the wood, Fox was getting ready to go out. He went to find his big bag.

"Where are you going?" asked his mum.

"I'm going to go to the very middle of the woods," said Fox. "I'm going to catch my dinner."

"Well," said his mum, "be careful."

Fox caught three grasshoppers and put them in his big bag. Then he went skipping over the grass.

Fox found six snails and put them in his big bag. Then he went jumping over the bracken.

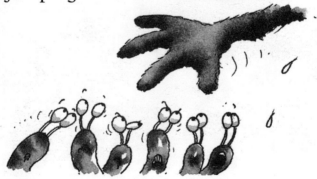

Fox snapped up eight wriggly
worms and popped them in his big
bag. Then he went hopping over
the brambles.

Fox reached the very middle of the woods.

"Well, well, well," he said. "What have we got here?" He looked at Hector and Hattie and Harry and Hester, and he tiptoed right up to them.

"BOO!" shouted Fox.

Hector and Hattie and Harry and
Hester woke up with a jump.

"Hee hee!" laughed Fox. "This
is better than grasshoppers or snails
or wriggly worms. Now, which of
you shall I put in my big bag?"

Hector and Hattie and Harry and
Hester looked at each other.
Hector winked at Hattie, and
Hattie winked at Harry. Harry
winked at Hester, and Hester
winked at Hector. Then they
looked at Fox.

"I'm fat," said Hector.

"But I'm fatter," said Hattie.

"I'm tasty," said Harry.

"But I'm tastier," said Hester.

They all held hands and danced in
a circle round and round Fox.

"All of us are rather fat,
None of us are thinner,
Hurry, hurry, Mr Fox
Come and choose your dinner!"

"Stop it!" said Fox. "You're
making me giddy."

Hector and Hattie and Harry and
Hester went faster and faster and
faster.

"Thinner, fatter,
Fatter, thinner,
Which of us
Is Foxy's dinner?"

Fox spun round and round in the
middle.

"Stop it!" he snapped. "Stop it!"

Hector and Hattie and Harry and
Hester went on spinning.

"Dinner, dinner, dinner, dinner.
Ready, steady, go!" said Hector.

They each spun away into the
brambles and curled up into neat
little balls.

"Oops, I feel giddy!" said Fox,
and he fell over in a heap.

"Ouch!" he said, and sat up. He rubbed his eyes and looked all around.

"No dinner," he said. "Nothing to put in my big bag." He rubbed his eyes again, and began to sniff and snuffle.

Hector heard Fox sniffing.

"Cunning little Fox," he said to himself. "He's trying his foxy tricks." And he stayed just where he was.

Hattie heard Fox sniffing.

"Cunning little Fox," she said to herself. "He's trying his foxy tricks."

And she stayed just where she was.

Harry heard Fox snuffling.

"Cunning little Fox," he said to himself. "He's trying his foxy tricks."

And he stayed just where he was.

Hester heard Fox snuffling.

"Poor little Fox," she said to herself. "He sounds so sad." She uncurled herself and ran over to see him.

"Don't cry, Fox," Hester said.

"I WON'T!" said Fox, and there wasn't a sign of a sniffle or a snuffle. With a bounce and a bound he pushed Hester over. With one pat of his paw he rolled her into his big bag.

"Grasshoppers, snails, wriggly worms and a fat little hedgehog!" said Fox. "What a wonderful, wonderful dinner I've caught!"

And he began to walk home,
dragging his big bag behind him.

Hector and Hattie and Harry
came hurrying out from under the
brambles.

"Quick!" said Hector, and they scurried after Fox.

"Mr Fox! Mr Fox! Wait for us!" shouted Hector.

Fox looked behind him. "What is it?"

"You haven't caught me!" Hector said. "I want to be caught as well!"

"And me!" said Hattie.

"And me!" said Harry.

Fox stopped and scratched his
head. "Are you sure?" he asked.

"Oh, YES!" said Hector and
Hattie and Harry.

"I don't think it's quite usual,"
Fox said. "I think you ought to
run away."

"Oh, NO!" said Hector and
Hattie and Harry.

Fox sat down to think. Hester poked her nose out of the big bag.

"Why have we stopped?" she asked.

"We want to come too," Hector explained. "But Fox doesn't think we should."

Fox shook his head. "I don't know what to think," he said.

"There's plenty of room in the bag," Hester said. "It's a very BIG bag."

Hector looked at Fox. "Will your
mummy be pleased if you catch
one fat little hedgehog?" he asked.

Fox nodded.

"Then," said Hector, "she'll be
VERY, VERY pleased if you catch
four fat little hedgehogs."

Fox looked more cheerful.
"Yes," he said.

Hector patted Fox's head. "That's all right then." And he opened up the big bag and walked in.

"Thank you very much, Fox," said Hattie, and she walked in too.

"Thank you very much, Fox,"
said Harry. He walked in after
Hattie and closed the bag behind
him.

Fox got slowly to his feet. He
thought about the four fat little
hedgehogs, and he licked his
lips. Then he took hold of the
big bag . . .

"OH!" said Fox.

"What's the matter?" asked Hector, popping his head out.

"It's too heavy," Fox said.

"Shall we eat the grasshoppers and the snails and the wriggly worms?" Hector asked. "That would make the bag lighter."

"All right," said Fox.

"We won't be long," said Hector, and he popped in again.

Fox sat down and waited.

"We've finished!" Hector called.
"Try again!"

Fox got up and took hold of the
big bag . . .

"Bother!" said Fox.

"What's the matter?" asked Hattie, popping her head out.

"It's still too heavy," said Fox.

"Ah," said Hattie, "you'll have to try harder." And she popped back into the big bag.

Fox pulled.
And he heaved.
And he heaved.
And he pulled.

He puffed.

   And he panted.

   And he panted.

   And he puffed.

And he heaved.

And he pulled.

And he heaved once more . . .

"It's no good," puffed Fox, and he flopped on the ground. "The big bag is too heavy."

Hector popped out again. "My word, Fox," he said. "You do look tired."

"I am," said Fox.

"Shall we take turns?" Hector asked. "You pull us, and then we'll pull you?"

"All right," said Fox. "And it's
your turn now."

Hector and Hattie and Harry and
Hester walked out of the big bag.

"Here you are," said Hector,
and he held it open.

"Thank you very much," said
Fox, and he walked inside.

Hector winked at Hattie, and Hattie winked at Harry. Harry winked at Hester, and Hester winked at Hector.

"Are you quite comfortable, Fox?" Hector called.

"Yes, thank you," Fox called
back.

Hector and Hattie and Harry and
Hester took tight hold of the big
bag. They tied up the top one
way, and they tied it up another
way. They tied it up with four big
knots. Then they pulled and they
heaved, and they heaved and they
pulled the big bag until it was
outside Fox's own front door.

"Goodbye, Fox!" they called. "We
hope you have a lovely dinner!"

Hector, Hattie, Harry and Hester
ran all the way home.

"Would you like some dinner?"
asked Hector's dad.

"No, thank you," said Hector.
"We've had it."

"We had grasshoppers," said
Hattie.

"And snails," said Harry.

"And wriggly worms," said Hester.

"Goodness me!" said Hector's dad.
"What a lot of things you caught
in the middle of the woods!"

"Yes," said Hector, "we're very
good at catching things!"

And Hector and Hattie and Harry and Hester all laughed and laughed and laughed.

ready, steady, read!

*Other books in this series*